SIMON & SCHUSTER BOOKS FOR YOUNG READERS • An imprint of Simon & Schuster Children's Publishing Division • 1230 Avenue of the Americas, New York, New York 10020 • Copyright © 2014 by Scott Magoon • All rights reserved, including the right of reproduction in whole or in part in any form. • SIMON & SCHUSTER BOOKS FOR YOUNG READERS is a trademark of Simon & Schuster, Inc. • For information about special discounts for bulk purchases, please contact Simon & Schuster Special Sales at 1-866-506-1949 or business@simonandschuster.com. • The Simon & Schuster Speakers Bureau can bring authors to your live event. For more information or to book an event, contact the Simon & Schuster Speakers Bureau at 1-866-248-3049 or visit our website at www.simonspeakers.com. • Book design by Chloë Foglia • The text for this book is set in Americana. • The illustrations for this book are rendered digitally. • Manufactured in China • 0417 SCP

10 9 8 7 6 5

Library of Congress Cataloging-in-Publication Data • Magoon, Scott, author, illustrator. • Breathe / Scott Magoon. — First edition. • pages cm • "A Paula Wiseman Book." • Summary: A young whale enjoys its first day of independence. • ISBN 978-1-4424-1258-3 (hardcover) • 1. White whale—Juvenile fiction. [1. White whale—Fiction. 2. Whales—Fiction. 3. Animals—Infancy—Fiction.] I. Title. • PZ10.3.M282Bre 2014 • [E]—dc23 • 2013017696 • ISBN 978-1-4814-0533-1 (eBook)

For Cecelia, Ella, Phoebe, and Piper

Breathe

Scott Magoon

A Paula Wiseman Book
Simon & Schuster Books for Young Readers
New York   London   Toronto   Sydney   New Delhi

Breathe, little whale!

Play all day

and swim,

and swim,

and swim.

Breathe.

Dive

down

deep.

Explore.

Make

new

friends.

Swim.

Listen to the sea.

Sing.

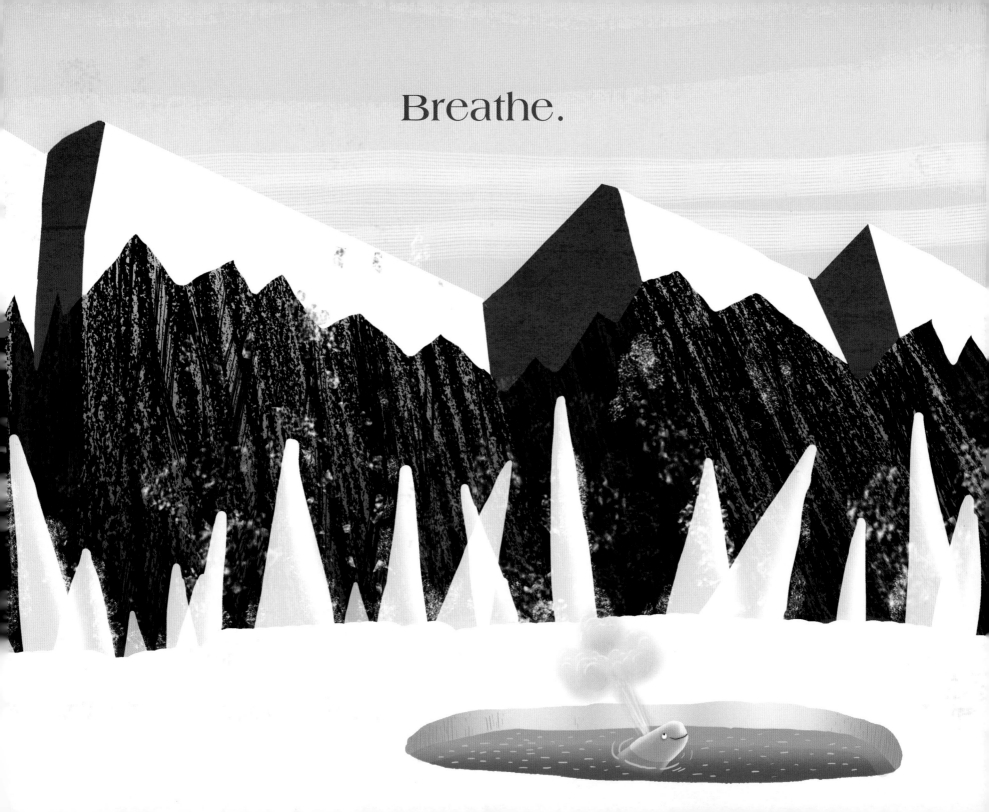

Breathe.

But fear not.

Find another way up.

Swim.

Most of all, love

and be loved.

Dream big.

Sleep deep tonight.

Breathe.

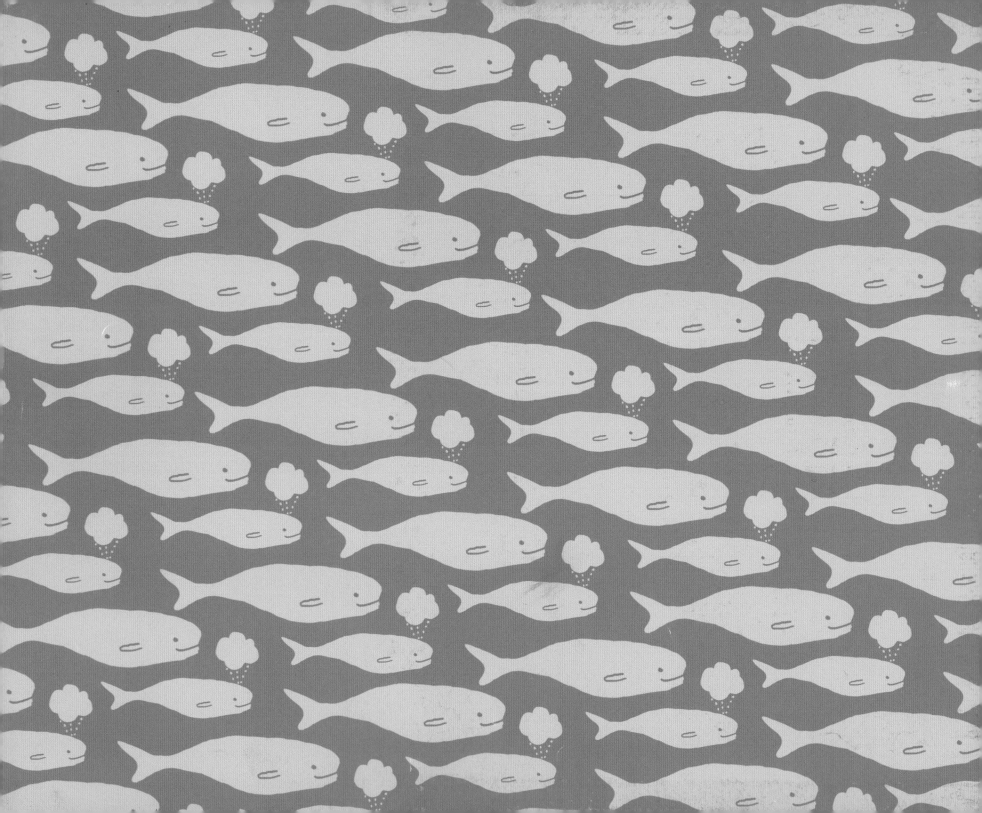